Contents

Meet Emily. Her grandfather owns Adventure Park. It's the best theme park in the world!

Meet Jacob. He's Emily's best friend.

Meet Frank. He's Emily's pet hamster.

Together, they test Adventure Park's new rides.

Some of the rides are magical. Some of the rides are scary. Some of the rides are dangerous. But ALL of the rides are exciting!

Join Emily, Jacob and Frank on the adventure of a lifetime.

Cast of Characters

Vocabulary

bandages – strips of fabric used to bind a wound.

pyramid – a building with triangular sides.

boulder – a huge, rounded rock.

shifty – looking dishonest.

CHAPTER 1 All Wrapped Up!

"It's got me!" Frank the hamster cried out. He was wrapped in a grubby old bandage and couldn't move.

"You're not the only one!" Jacob added. He was struggling with bandages of his own. The dirty strips of fabric were wriggling like snakes.

"I'll get you out," said Emily, rushing forwards.

Suddenly a hand slapped down on her shoulder.

"Leave them," hissed a voice in her ear. "We need to escape!"

"Not without my friends!" Emily insisted. "I've got to save them!"

But wait! We've missed the beginning of our story.

Why are Frank and Jacob wrapped in bandages and who is telling Emily to leave them behind?

Well, it all began when Emily, Jacob and Frank were helping out in the Adventure Park gift shop.

They were supposed to be wrapping presents, but nothing was going right. Jacob kept ripping the wrapping paper and Frank had got himself completely tangled in sticky tape.

"Get it off me!" Frank squealed. "It's stuck to my fur!"

"I'm trying," said Emily, snipping away with a pair of scissors.

At that moment, Albert Sparkle-Trousers rode into the gift shop on a motorbike.

Albert was Emily's grandfather and the owner of Adventure Park.

He also couldn't ride a motorbike.

He smashed through a display of mugs.

He crashed through a rack of t-shirts.

He ripped through a collection of posters.

Finally, the motorbike thudded into a pile of cuddly dinosaurs.

"Grandad, are you alright?" Emily asked, pulling a t-shirt off Albert's head.

"Don't fuss, dear," the old man said. "I've got exciting news! My new attraction is ready for you to test!"

"Oh no!" said Frank. "Things always go wrong when you open a new ride!"

"Not this time!" said Albert. "It's my best yet. In fact, you could say it's a-maze-ing!"

CHAPTER 2 The Pyramid

A few moments later, the children were standing in front of a massive pyramid.

"This is my Pyramid Maze," Albert said proudly. "It's the trickiest maze in the history of getting lost!"

"You expect us to go in there?" Frank asked.

The hamster had untangled himself from all the tape, but his fur was still really sticky.

"I need you to find the centre of the maze," Albert said.

"You mean you don't know where it is?" Jacob asked.

Albert shrugged. "I made it up as I went along. I'm pretty sure there's a way back out. Probably."

"This is a really bad idea," Frank said, leaning on Jacob's leg. "I'm staying out here!"

"Let's go!" Emily said and rushed into the pyramid. Jacob followed her. That's when Frank found out that he was stuck to Jacob's leg.

"Wait!" he squealed.

But it was too late. Soon the children were inside.

They ran through gloomy corridors. Flaming torches lit their way.

"I don't like this," moaned Frank.

They raced around a corner. A wall blocked their path.

"It's a dead end!" said Jacob.

"It's OK," Emily said. "We'll just go back the way we came."

But when they turned around, a new wall had appeared behind them.

"We're trapped!" said Jacob.

"Don't panic," Emily said. "It's not like we're standing on a trap door or anything!"

Without warning, the trap door beneath their feet swung open. The children tumbled into the darkness.

"Me and my big mouth!" screamed Emily.

Chapter 3 The Trap Door!

WAAAAAAH!

"Waaaaaah!" the children yelled. They were sliding down a steep slope.

"I hope we land on something soft!" Frank whined.

They fell off the bottom of the slope and tumbled onto a large, comfy sofa.

"Phew!" Jacob said. "That was lucky."

A voice boomed out of the darkness. "Beware the sofa of doom!"

"Maybe not so lucky," Emily shouted. "Get down!"

Darts whistled from holes in the wall and thudded into the sofa.

"It was another trap!" Frank squeaked.

"At least nothing else can go wrong," Jacob said.

The sofa of doom burst into flames.

"There's a door this way," shouted Emily. "Run!"

The three friends raced out through the door.

"It's just another corridor!" Jacob panted.

"Which way next?" asked Emily.

Frank pulled himself from Jacob's leg. "There's only one way to go. Straight ahead."

They crept down the corridor, hardly daring to breathe. The torches cast weird shadows ahead of them.

Emily peered at one of the walls. "Look," she said.

"There are pictures of crocodiles everywhere."

"Let's have a closer look," said Jacob and grabbed one of the torches.

"Don't!" said Frank. "You might trigger another trap!"

There was a rumble from behind.

The children turned to see a giant boulder rolling towards them.

"It's going to squash us," screamed Frank, running as fast as his little legs could carry him.

The boulder started to speed up.

"Quick," said Emily. "Jump!"

The boulder was right behind them. They threw themselves around the corner and bumped into two figures who were running the other way.

The boulder smashed into the wall, but the children didn't even notice. They were staring in amazement at the figures in front of them.

They were two huge insects!

The Tomb Robbers

"Who are you?" Emily gasped.

One of the insects was blue, and the other was red. They were both dressed in old-fashioned clothes and wore large hats.

"I'm Chirp," the taller, blue-faced insect said.

"And I'm Cheep," the shorter bug added. "We're tomb robbers."

"Er, he means explorers," Chirp said.
"Tomb explorers."

"What have you got in your bag?" Frank asked, staring at Cheep.

"Oh nothing," Cheep replied, looking shifty. "Just my lunch!"

"Yes," said Chirp. "It's not treasure we stole from the mummy!"

"M-m-mummy?" Frank repeated, his fur bristling. "What mummy?"

"Who said there was a mummy?" Cheep asked, giving Chirp a dirty look.

"He did!" Emily replied.

"Ha-ha," Chirp laughed nervously. "Don't be silly. There's no mummy in this pyramid. No mummy at all!"

Something roared behind the insects.

Something big.

Something big and covered in old bandages.

"Except for that mummy, of course," said Cheep, swallowing hard. "The one that wants to eat us."

"Because you stole its treasure?" Jacob said, looking up at the monster.

Chirp nodded. "Yeah, and now it probably wants to eat you too! Sorry!"

CHAPTER 5 The Mummy!

Everyone ran. In fact, they ran faster than they had ever run before.

The mummy chased after them. It was three times the size of the children and had a huge crocodile head.

"Where are we going?" Frank squealed. "All of these corridors look the same!"

"We hoped you knew the way out," Chirp admitted. "We're completely lost!"

The mummy snapped its jaws behind them.

Emily led them down a long line of columns.

"Around this corner," she said, but that only led to another dead end.

The mummy appeared behind them and roared.

"Quick," said Frank, "run through its legs."

But before Frank could escape, the mummy's bandages wrapped around him.

"I can't move," he squealed.

"Me neither," said Jacob. The bandages had twisted around him too.

"Wait a minute," Emily said. "I've still got the scissors from the gift shop!"

She pulled them out of her pocket and tried to cut the bandages.

"They won't cut!" she said.

"Leave them!" hissed Chirp. "We need to escape!"

"I can't!" insisted Emily. "They're my friends."

Jacob wriggled around to face Cheep. "Can't you just give back what you have stolen?"

Chirp nodded. "He's right, old pal. The game's up!"

Sighing, Cheep pulled a small wooden coffin from his bag.

The mummy roared in victory.

"It's still going to eat us!" wailed Frank.

"No it's not!" said a voice from inside the coffin.

Everyone stared as the box swung open to reveal another crocodile mummy. This one was much, much smaller.

"Now, stop all that noise!" the smaller mummy said.

The larger mummy fell silent straight away.

"Sorry Mummy," it muttered.

"What?" Frank said to the small mummy. "You're its mother?"

The smaller mummy nodded. "Yes, I'm the mummy's mummy and I'm very cross."

"Because Chirp and Cheep tried to steal you?" Emily asked.

The mummy's mummy shook her head. "No, because I've told my son no running in the corridors!"

The large mummy hung its head in shame.

"That's better," said the mummy's mummy. "Now, help these people find their way out of the maze before you get into more trouble."

The mummies led the friends out of the pyramid.

"Good heavens," said Albert Sparkle-Trousers when he saw the mummies. "What are we going to do with those two?"

"Funny you should ask that..." Emily replied.

Half an hour later, both mummies were happily helping out in the gift shop.

"What a brilliant idea!" said Chirp and Cheep.

Emily smiled. "Yes. Who better to wrap up gifts than mummies?" she said.

GIFT SHOP
£3.00

Questions

1. What did Albert ride into the gift shop? (*page 8*)
2. What did the children land on when they fell down the trap door? (*page 15*)
3. What happened when Jacob grabbed a torch? (*pages 17–18*)
4. What colour was Chirp? (*page 20*)
5. What did Cheep have in his bag? (*page 26*)
6. Where did the mummies end up working? (*page 28*)

SUPER SPACE ELEVATOR
DINO DANGER
JOUSTING DODGEMS
GHOST TRAIN
RIP
PIRATE SHIP
PYRAMID MAZE
RAINFOREST RIOT
RAINBOW ROLLER
ADVENTURE PARK
ADVENTURE PARK

Meet the Author

Cavan Scott spends his days making up stuff – and he loves it! He's written for *Star Wars*, *Doctor Who*, *Adventure Time*, *Skylanders*, *Angry Birds*, *Penguins of Madagascar* and *The Beano*! He lives in Bristol with his wife, daughters and an inflatable Dalek called Desmond!

Abby Ryder is a cartoonist who loves comic books and video games. Her greatest life ambition is to one day become best friends with a giant robot.